The Story of Heidi

Illustrated by Alan Marks

Retold by Susanna Davidson

Based on a story by Johanna Spyri

The wind whistled and sang.

    It blew in great gusts at Heidi and her aunt,

        as they battled their way up the mountain.

Up and up they went,

    to a world above the clouds.

At last they came to a small hut,
perched on the top
of the mountain.

A fierce old man opened the door.

"Meet your granddaughter!" said Heidi's aunt.
"I've brought her to live with you."

But I don't want her!

"I've looked after Heidi since her parents died.
Now it's your turn," her aunt declared.

And with that she ran
back down the mountain.

"Well, you'd better come in,"
said Grandfather, gruffly.

"You'll have to find your
own place to sleep though."

"What's up the ladder?"
asked Heidi.

Grandfather didn't reply.

Heidi climbed into a hayloft.

There, she made

a sweet-smelling

bed out of hay.

The next morning,
Heidi woke to the
sound of bells.

Sunlight poured in
through the window.

She ran outside onto the dewy wet grass,
where a boy was whistling.

"This is Peter, the goat boy," said Grandfather.

"Do you want to come up the mountain with me?"
Peter asked. "I'm taking the goats to find fresh grass."

Heidi went out with Peter and the goats every day.

In the evenings, Grandfather
fed her creamy goat's milk,
crusty bread and melted cheese.

"Read me a story," pleaded Heidi.

So, every night, Grandfather read her
a story by the fire.

Heidi had never been happier...
until one morning, her aunt came back.

"I've found a job for Heidi," she announced.
"I'm taking her to town."

"Poor Grandfather," cried Heidi.
"He'll be all alone."

"He likes it that way," said her aunt.

"He doesn't!" thought
Heidi. "One day I'll
come back to him."

Heidi's aunt took her
to a grand house.

There, she had to
look after a sick
little girl, called Clara.

"I'm so weak I can
hardly walk," said Clara.
"You'd soon get well
in the mountains,"
Heidi replied.

The town was full of jostling people.
Stale smells filled the streets.

NO
DOGS

NO
BALL
GAMES

Heidi longed for her hayloft,
for the jingling bells of the goats,
for stories by the fire...

At night, Heidi sleepwalked.
She wandered the house
in her white nightgown.

"That girl needs to go home,"
Clara's father decided.

A week later, Grandfather saw a strange procession coming up the mountain.

Heidi! You've come back to me.

"Clara wanted to come too,"
Heidi explained.

"Can she stay until she's well again?"

"Of course," said Grandfather.
"We'll help her get better."

Clara drank fresh
goat's milk every
morning, and
sat outside in
the sunshine.

And every day,
she walked
a little more.

"I can't believe it," said Clara's father,
when he came for her.

"Is this really my daughter?
How can I ever thank you?"

Clara... walking!

When Clara and her father had gone,
Heidi and Grandfather went outside
to watch the sunset.

"You're home now," said Grandfather.
"I'll never let you go again."

Taken from an adaptation by Mary Sebag-Montefiore.
Edited by Jenny Tyler and Lesley Sims.

Digital manipulation by John Russell.